MONSTAR
the Superhero

There are lots of Early Reader
stories you might enjoy.

Look at the back of the book or,
for a complete list, visit
www.orionbooks.co.uk

MONSTAR
The Superhero

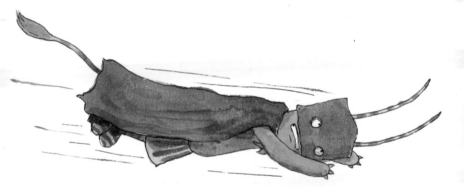

STEVE COLE

Illustrated by PETE WILLIAMSON

Orion
Children's Books

First published in Great Britain in 2014
by Orion Children's Books
a division of the Orion Publishing Group Ltd
Orion House
5 Upper Saint Martin's Lane
London WC2H 9EA
An Hachette UK Company

1 3 5 7 9 10 8 6 4 2

Text © Steve Cole 2014
Illustrations © Pete Williamson 2014
Inside design: www.hereandnowdesign.com

The Orion Publishing Group's policy is to use papers that are natural,
renewable and recyclable products and made from wood grown in
sustainable forests. The logging and manufacturing processes are
expected to conform to the environmental regulations of
the country of origin.

ISBN 978 1 4440 0972 9

A catalogue record for this book is available from the British Library.

Printed and bound in China

www.orionbooks.co.uk

*For Tobey - may you never
outgrow superheroes*

Contents

Chapter One

Monstar was Jen and Jon's pet.

She loved dancing, green porridge for breakfast and her blanky.

And her home at the bottom of the garden.

But most of all she loved Jen and Jon. And she loved everything they did too.

One day, Jen and Jon were
watching superhero films.
So was Monstar.

"I love superheroes," said Jon.
"Me too!" said Jen. "Let's dress up."
Jen and Jon ran to the dressing-up box.

For Monstar, the whole house
was a dressing-up box!

Making a cape from curtains was easy. Finding tights was harder.

A mask finished it off perfectly.

Monstar rushed to show Jen and Jon. "Look!" she said proudly. "Me **Super-Monstar!**"

Chapter Two

Soon Jen, Jon and Monstar were running around the house.

Jen and Jon's parents came out from their workshop. "Stop the noise!" moaned Dad. "We're trying to work."

"We're showing off all our gadgets at the town museum tomorrow," Mum said. "As soon as we finish our far-out flying boots."

Monstar jumped up and down.
"Super-Monstar **love** to fly."

"No, Monstar," said Dad. "These boots are **not** for monsters." Monstar sulked. "Not fair."

Jen patted her furry shoulder.
"Let's play in the garden. We
can make lots of noise out there."

But Super-Monstar was thinking
about the far-out flying boots...

Maybe they could make her into a **real** superhero!

Chapter Three

Next day, Dad drove the car to the museum with Jen, Jon and Monstar. Mum drove the lorry with all the inventions in it.

Jen turned to Monstar. "Jon and I have to help Mum and Dad. You can wait for us inside."

The museum owner did not look happy. "Pet monsters have to wait in a room at the back," he said.

Monstar curled up in the little room and waited…

And waited…

And waited…

After a while, Monstar decided to explore. She went out of the museum. Then she gasped.

Chapter Four

At the end of the street, some men were knocking down a house!

"Bad men knock down someone's house!" Monstar thought, and ran to stop them.

"Super-Monstar to the rescue!"
She jumped on the men.

"Stop!" A big man said to Monstar. "We are builders. No one lives in this old house. It isn't safe. We have to knock it down."

"Oh," said Monstar. She ran away.

She came to a crowd standing in front of a toy shop. Monstar joined them – and gasped.

A massive dinosaur stood there,
roaring and waving its head!

"Super-Monstar to the rescue!"

Monstar pounced on the dinosaur and dragged it to the floor. **Boing!** It fell to pieces.

A man rushed out of the shop.
"Oh, **noooo!**" he wailed.
"That was a special robot dinosaur!
It will take ages to fix! Go away!"

"Oh," said Monstar.
She was very sad. She hid in some bushes and didn't come out.

Chapter Five

Jon and Jen had finished helping
Mum and Dad.

All their inventions
were there:
Mum's robot
cleaner.

Dad's
porridge
machine.

Mum and Dad's far-out flying boots.

"Go and get Monstar," Mum told Jen and Jon.
But the little room was empty.

"Monstar's gone!" Jen cried.
"And it's getting dark!" said Jon.

"Oh, dear," said Dad. "Get in the car. We will look for her!"

The family drove all over town.
But there was no sign of
Monstar.

Jen wanted to cry. "What are we going to do?"

Chapter Six

Monstar walked through the
streets, looking for Jon and Jen.

She found her way to the museum.
The back door was wide open.

Monstar heard clanking noises. "Jon? Jen?" she called. There was no reply.

Then Monstar went into the large hall where Mum and Dad's inventions were on display...

And she saw three mean men who were stealing them!

"Robbers!" Monstar gasped. "This is a job for...

58

Super-Monstar!"

She jumped through the air
towards the robbers…

But went too far!

Clunk! Monstar landed right on top of the far-out flying boots...

And switched them on!

Chapter Seven

Whoooosh! The boots went whizzing about.

One of them kicked the first robber's bottom!

He went **splat** against the wall.
Monstar cheered.

The second robber tried to run.
But Monstar tripped him with
her tail.

He fell into the robot cleaner's arms. It tried to scrub him with a sponge! "Ow!" he cried. "Ooo! Get off!"

It looked as if the third robber would get away… But then the other flying boot hit the porridge machine – and turned that on too!

In seconds, the robber was covered in green goo, and slipping and sliding everywhere.

Suddenly the main doors opened
and Jen, Jon, Mum and Dad
came running inside with a big
policeman.

Mum and Dad turned off their inventions – and the policeman took the wet, wobbly robbers away.

"Monstar!" Jen and Jon skidded through the porridge to hug their pet. Monstar licked them both and wagged her long tail.

"We've been looking for you all over town," said Jon. "When we saw the lights on and heard crashing, we called the police. We're so glad you're all right."

The policeman smiled at Monstar. "This… *unusual* superhero saved your inventions."

Dad smiled. "Monstar, you really *are* a superhero."

"A *brilliant* superhero," Jen agreed.

"And the best pet in the whole world," added Jon. "Our very own, *super-duper* Monstar!"

What are you going to read next?

Have more adventures with Horrid Henry,

and travel the world with

Miranda the Explorer.

Play clever tricks with Twit,

spend Mondays at Monster School,

and even brave The Dragon's Dentist . . .

Learn how love is just like a Woolly Hat,

dance under The Little Nut Tree,

take home Monstar, the best pet ever,

and have an extra-special Mr Monkey birthday party!

Enjoy all the Early Readers.